De

-Second Edition-

Facebook: Kamille
Instagram: @iikamille
Twitter: @iikamillee

COPYRIGHT

Desperate Damsel 2
2nd Edition
Copyright © 2018 by Kamille Henry
All Rights Reserved.

Thank You so much for purchasing. I hope you enjoy.

-Kamille

Recap of Part 1

Eric had come home quite late tonight, but there was no surprise to that. He told Cynthia that we wanted to go for drinks and to get ready to leave with him.

When they arrived, the bar was crowded. Weaving their way through groups of people laughing and talking, Eric leading the way, they finally spotted the bar.

Cynthia looked around to see if Anthony was there, but she could see no sign of him. Reaching the bar, Eric asked for a bottle of red wine as usual. Cynthia hated red, and would have preferred a very light white wine, but Eric never asked her what she wanted, and the only time she asked if she could have a glass of white, he told her she was a heathen with no taste in wine and ignored her.

Grabbing the bottle and glasses, they made their way back to the group that Eric seemed to know, and she stood quietly with her glass of wine as the conversation swirled around her, headache increasing. Eric made a show of pouring everyone a glass of his expensive bottle and handing his wife his card from his pocket, he says,

"Be a love and go and get another bottle."

Slowly, she made her way to the bar where she stood trying to get the bartenders attention.

"Enjoying fronting for your husband?"

Cynthia turned her head to look at the person who had spoken in her ear.

"I beg your pardon?" Confused she saw that the person who had spoken to her was the girl she had seen with Anthony here a couple of weeks ago.

"Does your husband know?" and turning around to look towards Eric the girl said, "He doesn't look like the type to take it well, knowing his wife is screwing another man!"

Cynthia's face drained of blood, "I'm not!"

"Could have fooled me. You looked very friendly the other day. I'd say a little more than friendly."

Cynthia looked across at Eric, being the life and soul of the group and back at the girl next to her, watching her like a cat with a mouse, a hard look on her face.

"Well, bitch you're wrong. There is nothing between Anthony and me. He is just a friend. I hardly know him. So, stay the fuck away from me."

Cynthia may have been weak to her husband, but she was no punk to anyone else.

"Hardly know him. I saw you kissing!" Leaning across closer she whispered, "And he's very good isn't he. A very inventive mouth, and no inhibitions. Did you know that while he was screwing you, he's been making love to me?" Then leaning back, "Bet your old man doesn't do to you what Anthony does. But I guess that's why you're whoring out," and with a sarcastic laugh she walked away and over to where Eric stood.

Cynthia stood there stunned, her heart racing as she watched the girl now standing next to Eric, who was looking down at her with an angry look on his face. What was she saying to him? What if she told him that Anthony and she were having an affair? He would kill her. He would kill her if he even thought they were just friends.

Eric glanced back over at Cynthia with sinister eyes and Nicki grinned as she continued to stand next to him. At that moment, Cynthia's heart raced with fear. She wanted to run, but her legs wouldn't move. All she could do was stand there and nervously prepare herself for what was next to come.

Chapter 1

"What can I get you?" and she turned around, realizing that the bartender was asking her what she wanted.

Blurting out her order, she turned around to look at Eric and the girl. Relieved, she saw that she was no longer standing next to him but walking away and Eric was speaking with his friends and not glaring at her.

Handing over the card to pay and retrieving it back, she picked up the bottle and her glass, took a deep breath, and like someone walking over to their execution, went slowly over to Eric and his friends.

"What took so long?" he asked taking hold of the bottle while continuing his conversation.

Cynthia stood shocked still, watching him, trying to see what mood he was in with her, but he just carried on talking with his friends as if she wasn't there.

'Let the bitch sweat,' Nicki thought. *'The look on her face, it was priceless.'*

All she had done was say hello when she walked up to Eric, but Cynthia didn't know that. Nicki had no intentions of telling the bore about Anthony and Cynthia, yet. She wanted to let them worry.

When the time was right, she would let Eric know everything, and sit back and enjoy the fireworks.

*

Cynthia's headache was pounding in her brain. Everything seemed to be coming to a head all at once. She was finding it more and more difficult to juggle everything, Visiting Mrs. Brown and watching her deteriorate, dealing with Eric's increasingly erratic behavior, putting her escape plan together, and now that woman threatening to tell Eric lies about she and Anthony.

It all seemed too much, and as she lay next to her husband that night, she couldn't sleep. Worry swirled around her thoughts. It was all getting so complicated. The need to escape it all was getting stronger and stronger.

Where to run to, what to do, who could she trust? Years of not belonging as she grew up, and the years of her husband's abuse made her feel so isolated and the only people she felt she had any real connection to was Mrs. Brown; who was dying and soon be gone, and Anthony; who was the lover of that horrible girl tonight, and she hardly really knew him.

Chapter 2

The weekend came and went. Cynthia divided her time between the Senior Living where Mrs. Brown had moved to on Friday, and Eric who seemed to be in a good mood, treating her in a way she'd almost forgotten he knew how to do.

Going for a walk together, he talked about going away on holiday, and holding her un-bandaged hand in his, they strolled along, looking like any other young married couples.

As they sat down by the side of the river that ran close to the park, watching some children feeding swans and ducks, he seemed to be deep in thought. After a while, still looking at the children, he moved her hand into both of his in his lap and said,

"I know I've always said I didn't want children, but you know, I have been thinking, and maybe the time is right," and turning his head, he looked at her, "You could leave your job. The money doesn't really make much difference to us, and having a child would give you something to devote your time to,"

"I like my job,"

"You'll like having a baby. Besides, you always said you wanted children when we first married,"

"Yeah." She said dryly, but in her heart, she knew having a child with him would isolate her even more. No point arguing about it, he would just get angry. She was going to leave. Let him think she was agreeable.

So, they sat there as he talked about his plans for the future, and she listened. Just as she always did.

Chapter 3

Anthony felt his phone buzzing in the back pocket of his jeans telling him a text had been sent to him. Removing the phone, he looked at the screen. Seeing it was from Nicki, a deep frown formed between his eyes as he read:

Does her husband know you're fucking his wife? Funny how it turned out to be that boring bastard that brought us together. Damn, what a small world, don't ya think?

"What the fuck is she talking about?" He questioned aloud, aggravated as he re-read the text over and over.

He had deliberately avoided Nicki lately as he felt it would be wrong to string her along. She had seemed to want more from him than he was willing to give, and he felt bad about sleeping with her, especially that last time. Although they were both consenting adults, he just felt uneasy for some reason about carrying on with the relationship that she had seemed to think was a sign that they were together.

"What did she mean, *'does her husband know we're fucking?',* I'm not sleeping with Cynthia and why would Nicki care anyway?" he said out loud to himself.

He put the phone back in his pocket and picking up the remote control turned on the TV to settle back and relax to watch the football game, putting the text to the back of his mind.

Chapter 4

Monday morning as she alighted from the bus near the Senior Living, she saw him. A frown appeared on her face, what should she do? If she ignored him, she knew he would follow her and demand to know why she was not stopping to talk to him.

But he shouldn't have come to meet her here. He was complicating things for her.

As she approached where he stood next to his bike at the side of the road, she thought of what she would say to him. Not seeing him each day just for the small time they spent together, talking and laughing would be a real loss, a small time of being carefree in a life filled with fear and hurt, but if Eric ever found out, the problems and pain it would bring would be too much. Better to stop this now. Soon, she'd be gone anyway and he would be a sweet memory. Someone who had been a pool of sunlight during a bad time in her life.

Anthony could see by her solemn face something was wrong. Folding his arms in a defensive stance he waited for her to reach him. As she came closer, he could see the worry in her lovely eyes, her mouth pinched and tight.

"What's up? Want to tell me what's wrong now?" he could see she was uncomfortable. She was looking down at her feet, the road, people around them, anywhere, but at his face.

"Anthony, please stop meeting me at work,"

"Why? I thought we were friends,"

Pulling her jacket more tightly around her and looking towards the road she said softly, "But you want to be more than friends, and I'm married. My husband would be livid if he found out. So please, can you just stop this.

"Your husband?" and grabbing her arms he looked down at her, "What about us?"

"There is no us,"

He felt as if she had slapped him," Are you telling me you don't want me to see you at all anymore?"

"Yes, it would be better," she moved a step back and shrugged off his hands, "for both of us,"

And walking past him went through the gate of the Senior Living grounds and ran up the path to disappear behind the trees and bushes, out of his sight.

"So, you gone do me like that, huh?" he said to himself with animosity.

Stunned, he stood there not sure what to do. The last few months he had felt like he was on a rollercoaster running out of control. His feelings had become intense, but now he realized that the bond he felt was all one sided. He had become almost a stalker to the woman he loved. Wanting to see her may have made her life more difficult. She had never encouraged him, but his need had led him to push for more than she could give. So, what should he do now?

Chapter 5

Heart beating, Cynthia removed her jacket and hung it up in the office. Focusing on her work and her patients would be the best way to forget the mess her life had become, and walking into the lovely bright room where Mrs. Brown had been placed, she looked across towards the bed and a feeling of dread descended on her.

Looking down at the figure in the bed, breathing labored, sunken eyes closed, body so still, she sank down on the chair beside the woman now laying there in a coma, and knew the waiting time had begun. Cynthia stayed by her side for hours, forgetting about her shift being over.

***

Where the hell was she? He had arrived home to an empty house, no sign of his wife.

The little patience he had ran out after an hour of waiting, pacing around the downstairs of the house, anger rising like a wave in his stomach. The deal he was working on didn't fall through and his fragile ego was badly damaged. The tide of inadequacy washed over him and the need to lash out to get relief raised with every deep breath he took.

Grabbing his jacket and car keys, he slammed through the front door, and into his car.

"The lil bitch has been spending too much time lately with that dying old hoe."

And putting the car in gear he reversed out the driveway and headed for the Senior Living.

The young nurse first heard the noise as she stood by the medicine cart; a man's loud voice rang out through the usually peaceful and tranquil downstairs area. Quickly she locked down the cart and went to where the sound was coming from. A man stood, leaning in towards the owner, crowding her into the hallway wall, his voice raised and angry, his body language threatening, loudly demanding to see his wife. Shaking her head and trying to placate the man, the owner spoke quietly and calmly, but the man's demeanor seemed to tighten with every passing minute.

Turning on her heel, the nurse ran to the office at the end of the hall and picking up the phone, she began calling the police. Leaning across to the right so she could see through the door and down towards the unfolding scene she spoke on the phone, explaining to the operator what was occurring and giving the address.

Eric snarled at the woman in front of him, her dark brown eyes staring clear and calm into his hot angry eyes,

"Is she fucking here or not? I'm asking you one last time. Where the fuck is she, where is the lil ugly bitch?" and with a quick twist of his body, he stalked down the hall towards the office where the nurse stood talking on the phone, and then turned left into the spacious day room with its large plants, comfy chairs and large bright airy windows.

Startled patients and visitors turned towards the door as it banged open and the angry man stood looking around, eyes moving from small group to small group searching for his prey. With a snarl, he turned abruptly and half striding, half running followed the hall to the next door and opening it to look into an empty office filled with a desk and filing cabinets.

A blind rage had settled over him, and quite unusually, he was showing it in public. Normally, Eric showed the outside world a charming and controlled image, playing a role that he knew would manipulate and manage the people around him. All his life he had felt this need for the satisfaction of control. Unable to deal with anxiety and any feelings of insecurity or inadequacy, the outlet of the inner rage he felt had always been targeted towards the women in his life. But slowly the mask was slipping, the rage building, and the feelings of injustice becoming stronger.

Spotting the stairs leading up to the next floor he ran up, taking two steps at a time, and turning left ran up to the open door leading to a small two bed room where

Cynthia sat beside Mrs. Brown's supine body, holding her hand and whispering words of comfort as the old woman moved closer to her final breath.

Spotting his wife with her back to him, Eric walked up to her, past the curious looks of the other visitor sitting beside the patient in the other bed, grabbing her arm, pulled her up, and started to drag a startled Cynthia after him, causing her to fall to the ground as her feet failed to turn around fast enough to follow him.

"Bitch, get the fuck up and stop embarrassing me!" And with a hard yank on her arm, he pulled her back up and continued to haul the frightened and embarrassed female after him.

"Eric, please stop. Wait, my bag!" She stammered, looking back towards the bed where she had been sitting on the now overturned chair, her bag on the floor, the body in the bed laying quietly. Tears started to flow, and the dark cloud of humiliation and sadness swept through her body as she saw the horrified eyes of the people watching the scene unfold in front of them.

"Get your fucking bag and get your ass in gear," Letting go of her arm he turned and stood hands on hips, watching her as she scampered back towards the bed, bending over to pick up the chair and her bag, and then over the woman in the bed to give her a kiss on her cheek and whisper to her,

"I'll be back tomorrow, I promise, hold on."

"See bitch, now you're testing my fucking patience. One of these days I'm gone fucking kill your stupid ass!" And grabbing her wrist started to leave the room, pushing past the nurse and the owner standing there watching with growing horror what was happening to their colleague.

Chapter 6

Glancing at each other, the owner, Mary and the nurse, Jackie, followed Cynthia and her husband down the stairs as he pulled her behind him, never letting go of her wrist. Not sure what to do next, the two concerned co-workers followed, praying the police would arrive before the couple left. Both had seen the bruises over the years and guessed that Cynthia's home life was difficult, but talking with her about it had been rebuffed, and they had respected her privacy, while still being concerned and supportive. But now it was in front of them in all its ugliness and immediacy. As they reached the bottom of the stairs and started to walk towards the main door there was a buzzing of the front bell, and all four of the group, the two members of staff standing behind Cynthia and Eric, came to an abrupt halt.

"Excuse me," Mary calmly brushed past the now still couple, the woman looking flushed and distressed and the man with a scowl on his face. Walking to the door and opening it to find two young policemen standing there waiting, she drew a deep breath of relief.

"Good evening, I believe you called to report an incident?" the slim and taller of the two men asked. Looking behind Mary towards the couple standing there, and noticing the man holding the woman's wrist, and the look of distress on her face, he addressed Eric, "Good evening Sir, do you mind if we come in and have a small chat?" and both the Policemen stepped into the hallway and turning to Mary one of them asked if there were a couple of rooms they could use for privacy.

Pointing to the two offices, one that the original phone call was made in, and the office that Eric had first entered looking for Cynthia, "Yes, please use these. You will have complete privacy in them." Mary said, a serious look of concern on her face as she turned back towards Cynthia who now stood head bowed, shoulders hunched, her demeanor cowered.

The Policeman asked quietly if Cynthia was alright, and on getting a nod of her head, gently ushered her into one of the offices. Meanwhile, Eric was led politely to the other office by the one who had yet to speak.

Gesturing for Cynthia to sit down at the chair in front of the desk, and then perching on the edge of the desk the constable introduced himself as Victor Cray, "Vick to my friends," and smiling softly asked Cynthia her name, "Well, Cynthia could you tell me who the man you were with is, and if you are truly okay?"

In a quiet voice, looking down at her lap, her cheeks red with embarrassment, "Eric is my husband,"

"Are you hurt anywhere?"

"No,"

"Okay, what was the argument about?"

"I'm late home. I didn't call to let him know?"

"Does he get angry with you a lot if you don't let him know where you are?"

"He worries about me,"

"Uh huh. Does he lose his temper with you a lot?"

"Only when things build up at work. He's under a lot of pressure," and Cynthia looked up, pleading eyes fixed at the young policeman's face, "Please, I don't want to make this a big deal,"

"Cynthia, is this something that is happening a lot? Do you have a court order out against him at present?"

A small shake of her bowed head, and Vick lowered his voice to a gentle pitch.

"If it is and you need help, I can point you in the right direction. There are people who can help. Do you want to press charges?"

"Please, I just want to go home,"

"Are you sure you are alright, and that you want to go home?" Another nod of the head. "Okay, but I'll have a quick word with your husband first, and I want you to take this number and call it if you need help." Picking up a pen and paper he wrote down the number for the helpline.

Vick had seen a lot of domestic incidents in his three years in the force. He knew that the victims often didn't make the break until over thirty-five separate attacks, some of them involving broken bones, and hospital treatment. The women were just too scared to make the break, and although he felt something deeper was occurring here than just a general domestic, his hands were tied unless the distressed woman in front of him admitted to him and made a statement that her husband was causing real physical harm. But on the face of it, this call would just be a check that all is alright and a small warning to the husband, and then a logging of the call.

Asking Cynthia to wait in the office, Vick walked down the hall, stopping off to talk to the two women who stood there, asking what they had witnessed. After a quick chat and noting that the more senior of the two mentioned seeing bruises and marks on Cynthia in the past, and the threat in front of them all that he would kill her, he carried on to the other office where his partner, Peter was waiting with the husband.

Eric was standing chatting with the other policeman, all charm, working the man who stood before him, man to man.

"Hello, Sir. Can you tell me what just occurred?"

Smiling at the policeman that had entered and realizing that the best action would be to admit that he had lost his temper a bit but was sorry and was calm now he started to explain.

"Look, I'm sorry, I know it was wrong. I just had a bad day at work and came home and when my wife was not there, I started to worry. She's normally very punctual. As time went on, I really started to worry. You know how it is out there, dangerous, and I guess I just got a little too worked up worrying and over reacted when I found her. It won't happen again,"

"Well, sir I hope it won't, and I must warn you that this incident will be logged, and I don't want to be called out to you both later on tonight. Now you have found your wife, I hope you will go home and be a little more restrained,"

"Yes of course, now I know she is safe. You know how it is, a man worries about his woman and as I said, I just over reacted. Won't happen again,"

"Good. By the way, how did you get here tonight sir, was it by car?"

"Yes, I'm parked out in front,"

"Have you been drinking at all tonight, Sir?"

"Just the one at home,"

Vick looked Eric in the eyes for a long pause, assessing if the man in front of him was now calm and contained. He seemed contrite, and sincere, but Vick knew appearances could be deceptive.

"Stay here and I'll go and get your wife." and he went back to where Cynthia now sat, Mary and the nurse fussing around her.

"Cynthia, are you sure you're alright? How do you feel?"

"Yes, I'm fine, I just want to go home." and getting up she followed the policeman down the hall and to where Eric stood.

Chapter 7

The silence in the car was heavy with threat, and as she sat there unable to stop the quivering muscles and feeling of dread that ran through her body as they drove home. Eric for once, sticking to under the speed limit, his teeth clenched, his eyes glancing in the rear mirror as he watched the police car trailing them until suddenly, it peeled off down a side road leaving them five minutes from home.

"Bitch, you fucking, bitch. Embarrassing me like that!" keeping his eyes on the road in front he continued, "You spend enough time with that old crone, I expect you to be home when I get home," Looking sideways at the cowering woman beside him, "I expect you to act like a wife. Food on the table and sex in the bed. But you can't get either right, you stupid, ignorant, bitch!" As they pulled up and stopped in the driveway, he turned to her. "You are going to give up the job, have a kid, and take care of me. When you go in tomorrow, give your damn notice! I want you here where I know where you are. Not off somewhere looking after other people. I'm your husband and I expect you here. Do you understand?"

"Yes,"

"Good. Now get your stupid ass out of my car."

***

Cynthia lay quietly next to the sleeping man, planning and scheming in her head.

Grab a few necessary things, go to Mrs. Brown's house, dye her hair, put on the glasses and old clothes she had found in the bedroom, grab the new identity documents and she would be off. All traces of Cynthia gone, reborn as Kimberly Brown. Then she could pick up the lottery check and deposit it into the new account. Within days, she would be gone. Out of this nightmare and into the next phase of her life. No trace of her old self left for Eric to follow.

Chapter 8

Mary watched as Cynthia arrived and walk up the stairs from the office door.

"Cynthia, please, can you come here a moment?"

Slowly, Cynthia walked back down the stairs and to the office where yesterday the policeman had sat with her. She stood there in front of her Manager.

"I'm so sorry about yesterday, Mary. It won't happen again,"

"Cynthia, you know I worry about you. This is a place where we really don't need disturbances like last night, and I know it is not your fault. Please, tell me if you need help. I want to help,"

Collapsing into the chair by the desk, Cynthia sat there shaking her head, "I promise you I will sort it out. It won't happen again,"

"There are refuges for women who need to get away from abusive partners, Cynthia. I can get you into one. I have a friend who works in that field. Just say the word and I'll get her down to meet with you,"

Looking up at the worried Mary, Cynthia gave a wide smile, "It would be no good if I left him and stayed in the refuge. He would come after me there. I've heard of women that have ended up badly hurt or worse, dead, once their husbands have found out where they are. Eric would kill me if he found me there. I need to sort this out my way. I promise it won't happen again. I just need more time,"

"If you change your mind, let me know. In the meantime, is there anyone else you know who can help you? A friend or family member, maybe?"

Cynthia shook her head, and then looking up with a serious look on her face, "The only real friend I had I told to go away yesterday. It's complicated, but Anthony is just a friend. A really nice man, but someone thinks that he and I are having an affair, and I am scared they will tell Eric," And looking down again into her lap whispered, "And if they did, he would really kill me then," Then quickly looking up again at Mary said earnestly, "But we're not having an affair. Anthony cares for me, but were not having an affair, he's just a friend."

"Cynthia, you need to sort this out so that you're safe. Promise me you will sort this out,"

"Yes. I promise I will sort this out. Soon, very soon."

***

Cynthia sat in the office numb with grief with the last ounce of her strength totally depleted. After all she had been through; the fear and terror she had been experiencing increasingly at home, the emotional void her life seemed to have become, the ravages of her young dreams as they lay like shreds around her, that one small part of her life which gave her comfort was now gone. The affection and the bond that she had felt with Mrs. Brown had sustained her for the last six months, and now it was gone. Mrs. Brown was gone, the one person she had come to feel like family, the Grandmother she had never had.

She had been someone who cared about her because of who she was, not because they were being paid to care for her like all the others in her past. Sitting there in the office, the sobs shaking her slight body, the feelings of grief, loneliness and loss filling her up, her heart breaking, she was unaware of the concerned looks of Mary watching her.

The older woman had seen Cynthia cope with the death of her clients before, but never had she seen her react like this, and she realized that there was so much more involved in this display of grief. Mixed with the trauma of last night, the pressure the young girl must be under in her home life and the loss of her patient, the reaction was probably a release valve that had been ready to be let go of for some time.

Gently asking if there was someone that she would like Cynthia to call to take her home, Cynthia had looked up, tears streaming down her face, eyes red and confused, and shaking her head whispered, "No one, Mary. I have no one." The plaintive comment broke the caring woman's heart.

"Surely you know someone who would come, apart from your husband? How about the man you were telling me about this morning, could you ask him?"

"I told him to go away yesterday," and taking the paper tissue being offered to her by Mary, she sniffled and then continued in a small voice, "Mrs. Brown liked Anthony. She thought he was like her husband. She told me he was a good man, but I told him to go,"

The tears started to flow again as she realized that there had been someone who cared for her and she had stupidly pushed him away.

"Well, if he is as good a man as Mrs. Brown thought, he'll drop everything, come and get you and make sure you're alright. Do you have his phone number?"

Taking the business card from her bag on the desk, Cynthia handed it to Mary and watched with a pounding heart as picking up the handset her manager dialed the number shown on the card in her hand.

Chapter 9

It was lunchtime, and he was in the bar with the rest of the crew, listening to them talking and laughing, but he wasn't joining in. He gulped down the second half of his beer and putting down the glass, started to walk towards the bar to order another one.

"Hey Ant, you getting another beer? That was your third one, man. It's not like you to drink during the day?" Carl, his good friend and business partner asked him.

"Yeah, well it's not like me for a lot of things lately. So, I guess at least I'm being consistent," and he leant his huge 6'5" athletic frame against the bar waiting to be served by the young man trying to deal with the rowdy crowd of people to his right.

"Leave work for this afternoon, I'll pick up the slack. You are throwing too many back to be out there,"

"I'm a big boy now, I can look after myself."

"I'm not asking, I'm telling you,"

Anthony's body started to tighten up, ready for a fight, an outlet for the pent-up emotions roiling around in his body, when suddenly the phone in his jeans pocket started to ring. Reaching in, he pulled out the phone and growled into it.

"Yeah,"

An unknown woman's voice replied, "Are you Anthony Adams?"

"Yeah," and not taking his eyes off Carl, "Who's this?"

"My name is Mary Humphries, I work with Cynthia who's given me your number,"

Suddenly, all his focus was on the voice by his ear, "Is she ok? Is everything alright?" A feeling of dread ran through him, "She's not hurt, is she?"

"No, she's not hurt. But I'm afraid she's very upset. One of her patients has died, one that she's very close to and she needs someone to take her home,"

"Mrs. Brown died?"

"Yes, I'm afraid. On top of everything else, Cynthia has taken it very badly and she's given me your business card to give you a call. Would it be alright for you to come and get her and take her home? I would normally call her husband, but I don't think he'd be the best person to give her comfort right now,"

"I'm on my way. Tell her I'm coming," And with that he started to walk towards the door of the bar when suddenly a hand grabbed his arm.

"If you think you're getting in that car after drinking those three pints you had better think again," Anthony looked round at Carl who was holding his arm, "Wherever you're going, get a cab, Anthony."

"I can't wait for a cab to turn up; I need to get across town right now,"

"Then I'll drop you off there. But you're not driving,"

"Ok, I appreciate it."

And the two men walked out and got in the Dodge Challenger and drove through the lunch hour traffic.

***

Carl stood in the doorway watching as Anthony knelt next the crying woman as she leant into him, sobbing into the big man's shoulder. He couldn't hear the quiet reassurances that Anthony whispered into her ear, trying to calm the distressed woman who seemed to cling to him as if he was the last person alive, but by the body language of the two people, he could see a man in love and now had a little more of an understanding why Anthony had been so uncharacteristic today.

Whatever was eating into Anthony causing him to act out of character seemed to be linked up to this crying woman in his arms. He watched for a while longer and then looking across at the dark-haired woman also standing watching the scene in front of them, signaled to leave the room.

As they met up in the hall outside, Carl explained that he had given Anthony a lift over from work, but that he needed to get back to the site, so he was leaving.

"Tell Ant to take her home in a cab and not to worry about coming back to the site today. I'll make sure his car is safe at the house for him to pick up when he's ready."

As he held her, he could feel the tremors subside, the moist warmth of her breath warmed his neck, and her unique smell filling his lungs. A mingled feeling of sadness for her anguish and the stirrings of arousal fought inside of him. Just an hour ago, he had thought he would never see her again, and now he was holding her small frame against him and knowing that it was him she had asked to be contacted when she needed someone made his heart swell.

Slightly turning his head to kiss the side of her head, he whispered, "Cynthia do you think you can get up? I need to get you home,"

"I don't want to go home. Not yet," and slowly lifting her head from his shoulder sniffed and shyly looked into her brown eyes, "Please can you take me somewhere where we can talk, and I can think? Anywhere, but home right now."

Rising up from his knees and then taking hold of her hands, he pulled her up and tucked her under his arm, walking her out to the hall where Mary stood waiting.

Chapter 10

The cab had dropped them off at the park a few blocks down. Cynthia stood quietly as Anthony paid the driver sitting in the car, one hand resting on the top of the vehicle as he leaned down quietly talking with the driver.

In the cab, he had told her he was taking her to his special place, the place where he came when he needed to clear his head to think.

Walking along the path, in a companionable silence, her small cold hand tucked inside his big warm one, she looked up at the trees around them. Leaves in hues of brown and gold rustled in the soft breeze and crunched under foot as they made their way deeper into the wooded area. Suddenly they came to a clearing and Cynthia stopped walking, breathing in the crisp autumn air as she smiled and took in the spectacular view in front of her.

They were on top of a wide high ridge, with a stunning view extending out in front of them like a patchwork quilt. Here and there groups of houses nestled together like little dolls houses, surrounded by fields, and narrow country roads crisscrossed each other leading off to a small town far in the distance, and a river meandered across the scene, winding its way until it disappeared out of sight round the edge of the curve of the hillside.

Cynthia watched as a pair of riders on horses trotted across a large green open area below, looking like children toys.

Anthony lead her to a wooden bench and there they sat, in silence at first, drinking in the peace and tranquility before them. The only other person sharing this serenity was a middle-aged man walking his dog, a large brown pit-bull who bounded around his owners' feet, tongue lolling as he waited for a stick to be thrown in the age-old game between dog and master.

Picking up her hand and placing it between his two palms, fingers entwined, Anthony stretched out his long legs and leaned back against the seat.

Lifting her hand to his mouth, he kissed the back and said softly, "I'm so sorry sweetheart that she's gone, that you're hurting so much, but for her the pain is no more,"

"I know, but I feel like my heart has been cut. She was the closest I've ever had to a Grandmother. She was so good to me, and I'll miss her so much, Anthony," as tears filled her eyes, "I've never had that feeling of belonging before, never had the kind of memory of feeling safe within a family. She made me feel as if there was someone who really cared,"

"I care,"

She heard him, but continued without responding, "All my life, all I really wanted was to be part of a family, but somehow it's always out of my grasp,"

"It doesn't have to be," turning his body on the seat and placing his arm along the back of the bench, while still holding her hand with his other, "Cynthia, if you want to belong, I'll be there for you. You don't have to be alone or put up with being hurt. I'll look after you, I promise. And I'll never hurt you. You can come with me,"

"I hardly know you. I told you, I can't just move in with you."

"Yes, you can. You hardly know me, and I treat you better than a man you've known damn near your entire adult-hood. I'll sleep on the couch and you have the bed. You'll be safe and not alone, and I'll protect you and keep you safe. You'll never have to be afraid or lonely again,"

"It's so tempting,"

"Then, say yes,"

"I need to sort myself out, get my things together,"

"Does that mean yes?"

"It means I need to sort myself out first. Please give me a couple of days to organize things and then I'll call you,"

Anthony raised his hand and stroked her cheek, "Just say the word and I'll come and get you." Smiling he noted she had calmed down and the color in her face that before had been so pale now was looking back to the normal light-brown color. Gently he leaned in closer and watching her eyes he tenderly kissed her, an open-mouthed soft kiss, one of promise and so much more.

Sharing a smile, they quietly sat in a comfortable silence until Anthony said, "I told the cab driver to come back about now, so let's get you home."

Walking companionably back to the pathway and through the trees they reached the front entrance of the park and stood talking while they waited for the cab to return. As evening dusk settled in, an occasional car drove past until one turned in to the car park and pulled in next to them.

Chapter 11

Eric looked at the woman flirting with him again. He had come into the bar earlier than usual for a drink before going home and she had approached him straight away. What was she after now? He didn't trust her at all.

She seemed to be talking complete rubbish, asking him questions about his wife. He felt slightly uncomfortable, like there was a hidden agenda with this woman and he didn't quite get it, and now she was talking about that big bastard she had left him for that first night. What was she going on about?

Suddenly it started to dawn on him, she was hinting at something.

The rage started to build as he listened to her talking, saying nothing actually, but hinting at plenty.

The bar started to feel hot and too crowded as he listened, the noise around them making it difficult to hear everything she was saying, but the gist of it now quite clear. His breathing shallow, a flush across his cheeks he stared at the woman seemingly enjoying his reaction to her poisonous drips of gossip.

He was going to kill that bitch he was married to. There he was talking about starting a family, planning their future, working hard to support them, and all the time she was playing around on him.

***

Walking her dog along the road, Shelia, the neighbor watched curiously as the BMW pulled into the driveway, the husband emerging from the car just as a cab turned the corner and stopped in front of him by the curb.

As she watched his wife emerged along with a very tall, big man in jeans and leather jacket, the husband turned on his heel and strode aggressively over to the couple. Suddenly a heated argument broke out between the three people, with the shorter and slighter of the two men shouting that he should have guessed that his slut of a wife was playing around with trash.

Shelia stood routed to the spot as the drama played out in front of her.

The taller of the two men turned to the woman and seemed to be pointing towards the cab, inviting her to join him and leave, when suddenly her husband grabbed her arm and pushed her in front of him, manhandling her towards the front door of the house. The larger man followed seemingly remonstrating with the husband and trying to talk to the now crying wife, and suddenly the couple were gone, through the door as is was slammed shut in the face and he began banging and yelling.

Fascinated, Sheila stood watching as the couple's other neighbors came out to stand in the front garden, then walk over to the agitated man banging on the door. The cab driver, now out of his car walked over and joined the small group. Suddenly, the door opened, and the husband screamed that if they didn't leave he would call the police and again, slammed the door in the faces of the four people standing there.

Chapter 12

Anthony stood outside the house, a ball of panic in his stomach, his hand running through his head in frustration. Worry for Cynthia touching every fiber of his being, he stepped back from the door and shouted.

"Cynthia! Cynthia!"

But there was no movement behind the door, and the three people surrounding him kept trying to pull him away from the scene, telling him to calm down, but how could he calm down when she was behind this damn door with that bastard.

"I don't know what's going on here, but my advice is to leave it to cool down. Come back tomorrow and whatever's happening will be a lot calmer. Give the situation a little space."

Anthony stared at the cab driver, and then back at the house. He could see Cynthia's husband looking through the window with his arm around Cynthia, and he realized that his presence would just inflame the situation more, and that the cab driver was right.

Cynthia said she would think about moving in with him and call him. There was nothing he could do right now, even though he was worried for her and her safety, he remembered something that Mrs. Brown had said to him. The inner courage she would need to make the break had to come from her and that he should just be there for her when the time came.

Nodding to the man in front of him, he walked back to the cab and giving his address to the driver, the two men got in the cab and left the scene.

Cynthia stood there trembling. Eric's arm around her shoulder, holding her still against his side as he hissed in her ear.

"You lil bitch, so that's your bit of rough on the side?" and watching as Anthony got in the cab and it drove off, "Well, say goodbye to him my love, because if you ever see him again. I'll not only kill you, I'll make sure he has a bad accident and never walks again. Should be easy to arrange, just a swerve of a car into him and he won't look so tall sitting in a wheelchair,"

Tears ran down her cheeks as she looked out at the now empty street, and then she felt Eric's arm leave her shoulders and suddenly her head exploded in pain and she collapsed to the floor.

"Bitch, you stupid bitch!" he screamed as he bent over the figure on the floor hitting and slapping her around the head and face, easily getting past the feeble attempts that Cynthia put up to defend herself.

Grabbing her feet, he pulled the nearly unconscious woman across the room and out through the door to the kitchen. He picked up a kitchen chair and threw it across the room then continued to scream and abuse her as she laid on the tiled floor.

The wooden chair bounced off the wall, hitting her hard across her arm and side, a bolt on sharp pain lancing through her ribs.

"You think you can play around on me with that big pile of shit. Well I'll teach you both!" kicking the chair off her, he leaned down and pulled her up by her hair to sitting position and hissing in her ear, "You belong to me until I get fed up with you. Do you understand? You live by my rules, and if you don't, I'll make sure lover boy's life is hell. And I can do it. I have friends who can do it. Do you understand, bitch?" And with a mighty push on her head he got up and left the room as Cynthia's head hit the corner of the end cabinet and she passed out on the floor, blood dripping from the wound in her scalp where it hit the sharp corner.

Storming out the house, Eric got back in his car and headed for the bar. Red hot anger ran through his veins and as he drove, his hands tightly gripping the steering wheel, shouting out loud to the empty car, "Bitch. Bitch, fucking lil, bitch!"

Suddenly with a screech of wheels, he turned the car around and returned to the house, storming back into the kitchen, bending down to grab by the hair the now unconscious woman, and raising his hand to hit her again.

Realizing his hand felt wet and sticky, he held it in front of his face and saw the blood. The dawning washed like cold water through him that she was bleeding from her head and was unconscious, her limp body un-responding to him.

Sitting back on his heels, he sat watching her as she lay there not moving unsure what to do next, realizing that this time he might have gone too far.

After a while shaking and scared, he stood shakily up using his hand on the kitchen counter to steady himself. He quickly ran back out of the house and into the car. A drink, he needed a drink and then he would decide what to do next.

***

One glass of wine had turned into a couple of bottles as the nervous 6'2", dark toned man stood drinking unsure what to do, praying that she would be awake when he returned to the house. He couldn't call an ambulance as that would entail too many questions, the same if he called a doctor. Best to leave it and see what happens, she'll probably be okay when he returned home, and turning around to the bar with a trembling hand, held it at the bar man as a signal to order.

The barman looked across at the agitated man holding onto the top of the bar as he stood opposite him ordering another glass of wine.

Earlier in the evening, he had noticed the smears of blood on the man's white shirt as he had handed over the money to pay for his drinks. Shirt slightly un-tucked and tie pulled loose around his neck the man looked unlike his usual immaculate self when he normally came to the bar. Tonight, he seemed distracted and nervous. The barman assumed it must be something to do with the blood, maybe he had been in a fight, although looking at the man he would never have guessed he was the type to use his fists, he always seemed the glib type to talk his way out of trouble.

'*Just goes to show how wrong you can be about someone*' he thought to himself as he handed over another glass of wine and took the money, watching as the man shakily lifted the glass to his mouth and gulped down half the rich ripe red liquid.

Chapter 13

Anthony hadn't slept at all, and as he stood in his kitchen drinking another cup of strong black coffee, he steeled himself not to go over to Cynthia's house but to wait for a phone call. All night he had lain in his bed, his mind turning over with worry, aware that his presence would have inflamed any situation between her and her husband.

But the waiting would be hell, the need to go and see if she was alright had kept him awake until the first rays of dawn when he moved his tired body, readying himself for work.

Today he would get the bus, but there would be no Cynthia to wait for as he sat on the wall. Today he would go to work, collect his car and then later on, go over to the Senior Living and check out that she was alright.

Drinking down the last of his coffee and rinsing up the cup he turned around and surveyed the room with a critical eye. He hoped that Cynthia would like what he had done with his home; he could picture her here in the kitchen, the two of them working together in the evening preparing a meal.

Walking into the bedroom, he grabbed his leather jacket off the end of the bed and shrugging into it, grabbed his keys off the stand and ran down the stairs and out into the morning rain.

Chapter 14

Mary hadn't heard from Cynthia, which was not like her. If she was ill or unable to come in to work, she would always call, but today, she hadn't, and it was now late afternoon.

After yesterday, she hadn't expected the young woman to come in, but she thought she would have at least called.

Going about her duties, she wondered if she should give her a quick call, and walking into the office sat down at the desk. It was then she noticed the business card lying next to the phone, and picking it up, she placed it in the drawer, so it wouldn't get lost and she could give it back to Cynthia when she came in.

Just as she was about to dial Cynthia's home number the husband of one of the patients poked his head in the office and asked if he could have a quick word with her, and pushing closed the draw she beckoned the man in, and with a smile asked,

"How can I help?"

They then chatted for a while and he left the office, leaving the worried woman to her thoughts.

***

Stopping the car in the lot of the Senior Living, rain drumming down on him, he ran for the front entrance. Striding up to the door of the large building and ringing the bell, he waited impatiently, rain pelting down on his hair and dripping down his face.

After a while, the door opened, and Mary stood there looking up at him, a quizzical look on her face.

"Cynthia's not here,"

"How is she? Is she alright?"

"She didn't call. I expect I'll hear from her tomorrow. She'll probably come in then,"

Anthony stood there for a moment, unheeding of the rain soaking him to his skin, then without a word to Mary, ran back to his car and drove off, the only thought in his head that she hadn't called work or him. And he needed to know she was safe.

Arriving at her home, he stood looking in through the large brightly lit window at Eric, sitting relaxed watching the television as if nothing had changed.

Standing there watching, eyes burning red for lack of sleep and worry, his body cold and wet, his stomach tight from tension, he banged on the door.

"Open up!" he yelled while banging.

Eric opened the door with a deranged look on his face, "Explain to me why you are beating on my fucking door like the police?"

"Where the fuck is Cynthia?"

"Listen, it's clear you have lost your damn mind, so I'm not gone fuck you up. Now, I asked you to follow her, not fall in love with her. You chose to do some extra shit, so get the fuck out my face!" Eric snapped.

"That's because you had me under the impression that you were married to a sloppy ass bitch, not a delicate, beautiful woman that you were beating on!" And stepping close to his older brother, completely hovering over him, he said, "Now, I'm not your wife or those trained bitch ass niggas that you rock with and fear you, I will end you and you know it. So, I suggest you cut the macho talk and answer my fucking question," Ordered Anthony.

Eric smiled, not threatened at all by his overly grown brother, "I don't know. You tell me?"

Frustrated with Eric, Anthony pushed him, nearly knocking him to the ground and stormed inside the house.

"Cynthia!" he yelled as he went room to room, but there was no answer and no sight of her.

Heading back to the front, he watched Eric as she stood in the doorway grinning with his arms folded.

"Did you find what you were looking for?" he asked sarcastically.

"You killed her, didn't you?"

"Who, me? Oh no, I'm not that type of guy," He answered being more of a jack ass than he already is.

"If you've done anything to her, I swe-,"

"What? What you gone do?" Eric interrupted. "The only thing you'll do is finish what we both started or back to nothing I will put you! That business you own, that nice home and car you have, is because I got them for you! Now, don't think I can't just snatch all that shit away! Get yo big ass out my damn house and scavenger hunt for that bitch somewhere else!"

Anthony didn't say another word. He knew he couldn't risk anything until he found out what happened to Cynthia. He purposely bumped into his brother and left his home.

Chapter 15

Days went by, but no word from Cynthia, no phone call and no contact. He haunted her job each day, speaking with Mary, sharing their worry about the lack of any sign of Cynthia. He drove by her house daily trying to catch sight of her. Every five minutes he would look at his phone to check to see if a text or missed call had appeared but there was no message, no sign of her, it was as if she had disappeared.

Discussing what to do about it as they sat together in the bright day room, Mary looked across at the anxious man sitting opposite her. Voicing the unspoken thought that had hovered between them for the last half hour, Mary quietly said,

"I think it's time to contact the police,"

Anthony looked up, the feeling of real dread that had haunted him since that night he had left her behind now taking full grip and settling as a dark cloud draining all other thoughts.

"I should never have taken her home," his shoulders slumping further, his head bowed in defeat, "I was a fool, it's all my fault,"

"No, Anthony, it's not your fault. None of this is your fault. It was happening before you met her,"

"But I didn't help the situation. It gave him a reason. I love her so much it hurts, and I've done nothing but cause her pain and make the situation worse,"

"Anthony, listen to me, it's not your fault. I'm calling the police and asking them to go over there to check on her, but I want you to stop beating yourself up."

As she outlined what had occurred to the policeman on the other end of the phone, Mary explained that she knew Cynthia would have contacted her if she could have. Either because of work or because of Mrs. Brown's funeral, which was to happen later that week. Recounting the scene Eric had made the day before she disappeared, the person listening asked if she could remember the name of the policemen who had attended that night and assured her, he would get someone to go over and check out the situation.

Putting down the phone, she sat back and told Anthony, "The police are going over to check on her, and they'll let me know the outcome." But inside her heart, she felt the news would not be good.

A terrible premonition had settled over her and she worried how the man in front of her was going to take any bad news that might be coming their way.

Chapter 16

Vick stood waiting for the door to open, glancing to his left he noted the BMW parked in the driveway and stepping back, looked up at the light in the upstairs window. Raising his hand, he rang the bell again, wishing he was back at the station and out of this cold wind that had picked up during the day, and now in early evening, was whipping up and looked to become a real storm.

Deciding that there was no point is staying any longer, he was just about to turn back to the Police car when the door opened and, in the doorway, stood a very young woman with short black cropped hair, wearing a silky red Dolce and Gabbana gown.

"Good evening, is Cynthia Scott in?" he enquired, noting that this young woman was not the wife he had met last week at the Senior Living.

"No," the young girl hesitantly answered, pulling the robe higher across her breasts, and as she did so, Vick noticed the red marks around her wrist. "I'll get Eric," and she disappeared only to return five minutes later following the man wearing a red robe.

"She's ain't here," arms folded he stood in the doorway, his manner aggressive, "No longer living here. I kicked the bitch out,"

"Well Sir, can you tell me where she can be contacted? Do you have a forwarding address or contact details I can reach her on?"

"No, she probably toppin' off with that big thug she was having an affair with. I have no idea where they are, and I don't care. When you find her tell her she won't get a thing from me."

Vick looked behind Eric to the young girl hovering behind him and quietly asked, "When did she leave Sir, what date?"

"The 3rd, last week,"

"Thank you for your time. And if you hear from her, please can you get her to contact the Station and let us know, as we would like to confirm her whereabouts."

Turning and saying goodnight as he left, Vick had a bad feeling about this. He knew from speaking to the Senior Living Owner that she was not with the man that the husband alluded to, and he knew there was no sighting of her from work.

The door had slammed behind him and he was about to get in the car when he could hear a woman's voice calling out. Looking up, he noticed the next door neighbor standing in her doorway gesturing for him to come and speak to her. Closing the car door and walking over to the neighbor, he passed through as she opened the door wider and beckoned for him to come in.

After settling on the couch, the nervous woman started to explain that she and her husband had lived next door since the couple had moved in a few years ago and during that time, she had heard and witnessed some terrible scenes where the husband had terrorized the young wife, and recently the violence she heard through had increased until last week.

Last week, the night of the big argument in the street, had been the last time Cynthia had been seen or heard by her, or her husband.

"That night, my husband and I could hear him screaming at her. He screamed he was going to kill her. I was so worried, I wanted to call the police, but my husband kept saying to leave it alone, that it's not our business, but I'm so worried about her. There's been no sign of her since that night. And now he has that other woman living in the house with him. Yesterday, I noticed her wearing some of the wife's clothes when they went out,"

"When did the other woman move in?"

"About five days ago," Sheila answered.

"Tell me about the night of the fight in the street, what exactly happened?"

Leaning forward, relieved at last to be able to tell the Police everything she had heard and seen, Sheila Shaw poured out the story of her next door neighbor's turbulent marriage and the terrible things she had heard.

Chapter 17

He had no proof, just a suspicion built on intuition, but he felt that was enough to have a chat with one of the detectives back at the station.

Standing there leaning against the messy file covered desk, he outlined what he knew and felt. It wasn't much, but as he explained his gut feelings, Detective Alan Hudson listened intently.

"What do you think has happened?"

"Not sure, but no one has seen her since that night. Her manager says she knows she would have contacted her work because the old woman's funeral is within days and Cynthia loved the old woman,"

"You sure she's not with the boyfriend or that he's involved in anyway?"

"No, she's not there; he's pretty worried about her as well. Seems that no one has seen or heard from her, not the neighbor, not work, not her friends, nor does the husband seem particularly worried,"

"Maybe she ran off, just had enough of them all," said Detective Alan Hudson.

"Maybe, but I don't think so, though, not from what I witnessed. Seemed to me she was too cowered and too afraid of her husband to fight back, even to the extent of running. Alan, I just have a bad feeling about this. The husband is an arrogant son of a bitch, full of himself and if that night he went too far we might have a missing wife and only the word of the husband that she ran off,"

"Okay, I'll do a little digging, but I bet she turns up at the boyfriend's pretty soon," Detective replied.

"Just trust me, my gut never lies." Said Vick.

Chapter 18

Tapping the pen in his hand on the table in front of him, the Detective sat back pensively studying the man sitting opposite him in the interview room. He still wasn't completely convinced this person wasn't somehow involved in Cynthia Scott's disappearance. And it now was classified as a missing person case.

After a month and no sign of the young woman, no sign of her using her bank account, no sightings or contact with former associates, it was looking more and more like a case of foul play, but by whom, and when?

"Let's go through it again. You left in the cab that night and went straight home, no witness other than the cab driver, and no contact with Cynthia Scott from the moment you saw her go into her home with her husband?"

"Yeah, the cab driver took me back to my house." Leaning forward elbows on the table, he closed his eyes and recited again for the Detective in a hollow voice, "My car was taken from the bar where I had left it at lunchtime. An employer of mine had it driven to work where I picked it up the next morning," and looking up, "You can check with him, the car was at the site when he got in that morning and I came in after him, I was running late due to getting the bus and because of not sleeping the night before with worry about Cynthia,"

"If you were worried about her, why did you leave her behind?"

"I told you, her husband hustled her into the house before I had a time to react. I tried to get her to come out, but some people, the cab driver and some others told me to go as I was making a scene. I thought she would call me the next day and come and live with me. I was stupid, I shouldn't have left her. It's all my fault,"

"Mr. Adams, how is it your fault?"

"Because I knew her husband was abusing her, I had seen the bruises and marks over the past months. My being there, it just inflamed the situation," and placing his head down on his arms on the table shook his head against them mumbling, "And now he's probably gone too far and killed her and it's all my fault."

"Let's start at the beginning again. When did you first meet Cynthia Scott and where?"

***

At the case meeting, Alan reviewed the facts so far with the rest of the team.

"After speaking with the bartender where the husband visited later that night, I am now inclined to get a search warrant and bring him in for questioning," Alan told them.

"You say the bar man saw blood on his shirt? How much blood?" Vick asked.

"Smears, but enough to be suspicious. He could have killed her, gone back after getting drunk enough to have the courage to deal with the body, and got rid of it that night or during the next day. The guy says he was very agitated, unlike his normal self, and work says he was off that next day. Plenty of time to get rid of a body and clean up any mess," Alan answered.

"Well that's it! Let's go!"

"We have to wait for the warrant to clear, Vick. Then we're in. Alan told him.

"At least let get his ass in for questioning. I don't like the fact that he's just brushed this shit off like he has no worries!" Vick said getting up from his seat.

Chapter 19

Eric sat waiting in the small room, his lawyer sitting to his left. The last couple of weeks had been hell. All around him colleagues and acquaintances had been questioned by police, then staring and talking about him. Each time he walked in a room at work, they all stopped talking and yesterday when he walked in the bar, he could swear every eye was on him.

It was becoming untenable. The bitch was making his life a nightmare more that she wasn't there.

Suddenly, the door opened, and two Detectives entered the room, one portly with a shaven head and black moustache under a big hook nose, the other looking more like a school teacher with silver hair and a scholarly air about him.

Sitting down, they introduced themselves and after explaining the procedure of taping the meeting and his rights.

The one with the silver hair, called Detective Noir, asked, "When was the last time you saw your wife?"

"The night I put her out, December 3rd,"

"Well Eric, can you tell us what she said when she left?"

"Nothing, she was gone when I got back,"

"Can you describe what occurred earlier that evening? What caused you to throw your wife out of the home you share?"

"The lil bitch came home with her boyfriend. I went outside to see what the hell it was about, sent him off and put her out, then went to the bar. When I came back home, she was gone. End of story,"

"So, what you are telling us is, that at no time after you entered the house did you argue or fight with your wife? What you are saying is that you asked her to leave, went out and when you came home, she was gone?"

"Yes, that's it exactly. The hoe was gone. Go speak to the boyfriend; he should know what happened to her,"

"Can you explain why your neighbor has told us she heard you screaming at your wife that night after you entered the house, and I quote, "*He screamed over and over, I am going to kill you,*" while she could hear your wife begging for you to stop hitting her. Can you comment on this?"

Eric sat back in his chair stunned. "I just said it, I didn't do it. I was angry. I had just found out she was two timing me. It was just words."

And for the first time, he realized he was in trouble.

Chapter 20

The week had been eventful for the investigation, with more and more evidence mounting up against the husband, except they had no body.

Standing in front of the team in the squad room, Alan shook his head, slouched with hands in his

"The traces of blood found on the kitchen knife makes me think she was stabbed. The blood smear on the steering wheel of the car makes me think he took the body and dumped it somewhere during the night," Alan spoke out to the group of detectives.

"Yes and even though he washed the dish towel, the blood stains on it shows he tried to clean up the mess with it, so I think she was killed in the kitchen," Another detective chimed in.

"He must have leaned against the kitchen counter, his bloody finger print and palm print showed up when the counter was tested by forensics. Proving he had access to her body after she was wounded," Said Vick.

"But is this enough to charge him? With no body, it's all speculation," Alan said.

"We need enough strands of circumstantial evidence to be able to charge him. Firstly, the hospital has past records of a broken wrist, the kind of break that can only be caused by rough twisting of the arm. Next, we have witnesses to other instances of abuse, escalating in violence and time between each one. The neighbor, the boyfriend, his and her work colleagues all witnessed signs of abuse, including bruises and cuts. His story keeps changing, firstly he told her to leave, next he came home, and she had gone. And don't forget the threats to kill her repeated in front of her manager at the Senior Living and heard by the neighbors," Said Vick.

"Also, what woman leaves her home without taking her bag, her purse, her keys or any make up or clothes?" Detective Peter said.

"No sign of movement in her bank account, she hasn't collected her last month's pay, no sign or sighting of her since the 3rd. The new girlfriend, Michelle is now living in her house and wearing her clothes," Said Vick.

"What about the boyfriend? The motive for Eric to kill her was she was going to leave the husband for him, the husband's ego couldn't take it. There he was a successful man and she was leaving him for someone he saw as below him in every way. What did he call him in the interviews?" asked the other detective.

"Her bit of rough, the big thug. All derogatory names. He felt she had slighted him, insulted him, and defied him. He hit out at her as he always had, and in his anger went too far. They were in the kitchen, he picked up the knife and then when he had realized what he had done, covered up. Moved the new girlfriend in and told everyone she had left him," Said Alan.

"But is it enough to charge him?" asked Peter.

"Let's dig a little deeper, see what else we can uncover." Alan answered.

Chapter 21

Anthony had retreated into his house, unable to work, to eat, to go outside where people went about their daily lives, laughing and doing the day to day things that people do.

He sat there staring ahead through dry, heavy eyes, seeing nothing except the pictures his mind conjured up.

Over the past weeks, he had hardly eaten or slept, and his face and body had started to show the loss of weight, and the lack of sleep etched deeper lines into the already deep creases that normally framed a smiling mouth, but now framed a mouth that reflected deep pain.

He felt he was going mad, each time he closed his eyes, he pictured Cynthia. He could see her smiling up at him, her beautiful eyes sparkling with amusement as he told her outrageous stories about himself. Her sweet oval face framed by that long silky hair, her gentle smile, only to be suddenly replaced in his imagination as dead and battered, her eyes closed, her face bruised and still.

Blame and guilt sat with him continually, turning over in his mind what he should have done, what he didn't do, how he should have seen this coming.

The police had interviewed him four times now, and although they seemed to have ruled him out, he still felt responsible, still felt that if he had just carried on loving her from afar instead of knocking on that door and getting to know her, none of this would have happened. He knew his brother was capable of many things and killing his wife was surely one of them.

Seven weeks had gone by and still the pain was as raw as it had been that first week. Would this pain ever leave him? He didn't really want it to, as he saw it as his punishment, his cross to bear for causing the death of the woman he loved.

***

Carl sat on the couch opposite Anthony, shocked at his appearance. The last seven weeks he had been off site, sitting here locked within his grief, but now Carl felt was the time to pull him out into the world, to face up to life, and he was not above a little manipulation to ensure it happened.

"As far as I can see it you have two choices, get back on site and finish our contract or I get the lawyers involved and you end up with high legal costs, your name blacklisted in the industry and possibly losing your home. Choice is yours,"

"You could get someone else to finish the job. There's plenty of others out there,"

"No one is as good as you, besides the contract is with us and our company, Anthony. We need to get finished on time or we'll go into penalty phase, and that will cost me, and if it costs me, it will cost you. We're in business together, but I won't taint my name because you are being irresponsible,"

Anthony sat scowling at this man who was threatening him; teeth clenched, a muscle jumping in his jaw as he contemplated hitting him to relieve his anger.

Rising to his feet, Carl grabbed his jacket off the couch and as he walked towards the door, he stopped and looked back down at the man sitting tense and angry and issued the warning.

"I expect to see you at the site tomorrow morning at eight sharp. There is a couple of sash window frames you were last working on, you'll find them propped up in the third-floor bedroom ready for you to start on," walking to the door he turned around one last time, "And Anthony, leave this pent up anger at home when you arrive." And then he was gone.

Chapter 22

"Look, Mr. Scott, it's inevitable we'll uncover everything. It's best you tell me the whole story in your own words. I understand you can love someone and still hurt them, she made you feel a fool, she was seeing someone behind your back, you were angry, your anger got the better of you and you lashed out. It was a crime of passion so to speak, not planned, spur of the moment, admit it and get it off your chest," Detective Alan told him as he slapped the evidence he found in his home on the table.

Looking at the pictures, Eric panicked and started talking.

"I admit, I hit her, she was unconscious when I left her, but she was alive. When I came back, she was gone,"

"So you admit you hit her?" Alan asked for clarity.

"Yes. I hit her," Eric admitted.

"You admit you hit her so hard she was unconscious?" Alan asked.

"No, when I hit her, she hit her head on the counter. I didn't knock her out, hitting her head knocked her out," Eric responded, now nervous.

"But you didn't call for an ambulance? Get help?" Alan asked already knowing the answer.

"No, but she was alive. When I went out, she was alive," Eric said, now sweating.

"Your wife was unconscious, so you decide to leave and go to the bar?"

"Yes. I know it sounds crazy, but yes, I left her there, but I promise she was alive,"

"Eric, explain to me the traces of your wife's blood on the knife, on the dish towel and in the plug hole?"

Eric paused and dropped his head, "I can't explain that."

**

Victor Cray looked up as Alan Hudson came in, a big smile on his face, "We've got him. We've got the bastard!"

"Now don't tease me, Alan. What have we got?" the Detective started to get up, people were streaming in through the office doorway, big smiles on their faces.

"They've found what they think are her clothes, dumped in an old building site not far from the railway station," Alan answered.

"YES!" and with a raised fist in the air the usually reserved Detective gave a big whoop.

"They're sure it's her clothes?" Vick asked.

"Yeah, they fit the description given by the boyfriend last time he saw her after he dropped her back home. And there's more," Alan said.

"What?" asked Vick.

"The jacket has blood all down one side, they're gonna to do the DNA tests against the hairs gathered from her brushes, but it's hers, I know it. We've got him," Alan cheered.

"How far is the dump site from the house or the bar?" Vick asked.

"It's on the way between the house and the bar. Five minutes from the bar I'd say," said Alan.

"Any sign of a body?" Vick poured out with another question.

"Not yet, but it's sure to be only a matter of time."

Chapter 23

Anthony stood in the hall, his heart beating so hard he thought it would explode out from his chest. He could feel the bile rising in his throat as he stood staring at the closed door.

The detective touched his arm and moved forward to open the door inviting him to step through, but he just stood there, rigid with fear, unable to move his feet.

"Mr. Adams, I understand this is difficult for you, but we need confirmation that these are the clothes you last saw Cynthia Scott wearing that night. We need you to do this for Cynthia. The case against her husband is building, but we need confirmation that these are her clothes. Please step through the door and help us to identify them."

Anthony looked back at the Detective, and then as a big hand had given him a push, he moved forward into the room. He stood looking down at the large table where items of clothes were laid out in their protective see through bags.

Unable to speak, he stared down at the white jacket he had so often seen her wear now laid out, crumpled and dirty with dark brown stains marring one side. Slowly the tears he had been holding back for weeks fell, as his large frame crumpled to his knees, the sobs started to wrack his body.

Alan looked compassionately down at the distraught man in front of him. Since first meeting him, he had come to realize that this large, tough looking man had been deeply in love with the victim, and any glimmer of hope she was alive had now been stamped out.

"Mr. Adams, please can you say if these are the clothes you last saw Cynthia wearing December 3rd?"

"Yes," looking up with tear stained face, "Yes, these are Cynthia's things, and I'm going to kill that bastard myself!" Anthony starred at him with pure anger in his eyes.

***

Anthony sat at the bar, hands shaking as he lifted the whisky up to his mouth. Unable to wipe the picture of Cynthia's clothes spread out on the table, the unmistakable stain of blood on the jacket, he closed his eyes, the mixed feelings of grief and anger swept through him.

After he had been ushered out by the Policeman and taken to another room to give and sign his statement, he had been warned not to go near Cynthia's husband and to leave it to the Police to deal with him. Anthony had stared long and hard at the cop, who reiterated the statement.

"Mr. Adams, if you interfere in anyway with Mr. Scott, we will be forced to arrest you. Leave it to us, we know what we are doing, and you will only cause problems with the case. The best way to ensure that Cynthia's killer is brought to justice is for you to tell us everything you know and give evidence at any trial,"

"But what if you don't get enough evidence to take him to trial? What if he gets away with killing her?" Anthony asked.

"We are building a case and there will be enough evidence, so long as you don't do anything stupid, we'll be fine."

It took him a moment to even take in all that happened not even an hour ago. Standing there in the bar, he finished off the last of the golden liquid in his glass, then caught the eye of the barman, signaling for another, when he felt an arm slide round his back.

Looking next to him, he saw Nicki, "Hi, want to buy me a drink, Anthony?"

"Just leave me alone, Nicki."

"Leave you alone? Why? Now that your little girlfriend is missing, I would have thought you wanted some company? It's been a while since you called me, a phone call would have been nice,"

"I told you leave me alone, I'm not in the mood for any games," He tossed the money on the counter and picked up the fresh drink, taking a long sip.

"Games, Anthony? I'm not the one playing games. Seems to me the two of you were playing games long before you and I met,"

"What the hell are you talking about?"

"I saw you outside your house with her, kissing. You told me there was nothing between you and her, that she was married. But I saw you, and you were more than just good friends, Anthony. You looked a lot more than good friends,"

"What the fuck are you saying?"

"You were having an affair, and that's just what I told her husband, just how friendly you and that hoe were,"

"You what?" he exploded, the whole bar got quiet as he stood, his body rigid with fury, the glass in his hand slammed down on the bar. Taking steps backwards, Nicki realized she had gone too far in taunting this normally laid-back man and looked up apprehensively at piercing eyes staring at her with pure hatred, "You simple, desperate, dumb ass bitch!"

Anthony started to raise his hands as if to seize her, taking a step forward, only to find his arm grabbed by his friend Carl.

"Leave it, Anthony, she's not worth it,"

"Not worth it? This raw pussy having ass bitch may have lit the fuse that killed Cynthia!" Anthony shouted.

Scuttling backwards she shouted back, "He was already hitting her, everyone knew! I didn't do anything except tell him about the two of you and what you were up to!"

"Man, if ya'll don't get this bitch!" he roared trying to release his arm from Carl's strong grip.

"Get out of here, Nicki!" Carl hissed, moving in front of Anthony and pushing him backwards, "Get out of here and don't bring your messy ass back!"

And she turned and ran out the bar.

Chapter 24

Michelle trembled as she was asked the questions by the female Detective, unsure what to say, and if any answers she haltingly gave was what they wanted to hear.

"When Eric gave you the skirt and top to wear, what did he say?"

In a quiet almost whisper she replied, "That he wanted to see me wear them,"

"Did he say why?"

"He said I would look better in them than his wife,"

"Did he say where his wife was?"

"Yes, he told me she was with someone else,"

"Someone else, did he say who?"

"No, just that she was with someone else,"

"Alright, let's talk about what happened when you put on the clothes,"

"He seemed to change,"

"Change? In what way?"

Looking embarrassed, she looked down at the hands in her lap, the top of her black hair was all the detectives could see as they heard an even quieter, "He screamed at me, called me a bitch, twisted my wrist and told me I was a slut," the young girl looked back up, her eyes wet with tears and reflecting her humiliation, "He seemed to think I was his wife; he called me Cynthia and told me I belonged to him. I was scared, but afterwards, um, after you know. Afterwards he apologized and told me he was sorry. That I was better than her, and he loved me,"

"Did this happen more than once?"

"No, just that one time, but he seemed to always want me to wear her clothes. During the two weeks I stayed at the house, he seemed to want me to wear her clothes all the time."

***

Sheila walked out of the Police Station into the cold crisp daylight. Giving her statement had taken most of the day, and sitting in the little room, telling the policeman all she remembered had made her annoyed with herself for listening to her husband and not taking action before.

Listening to herself list all the times she had heard the poor woman being screamed at, all the begging she had heard for him to stop hitting her, the bruising she had witnessed, she wished she could turn back the clock and offer the young woman support, and a lifeline. But now it was too late, but she would help to get the bitch of a husband by telling all she had heard and help to build a case against him.

It might be too late to save the young woman, but she was determined to make up for her keeping quiet and get revenge on the husband.

Chapter 25

Eric had been charged and was now on remand, the legal justice system was moving slowly, but inexorably towards the trial due to be held later in the year. Newspapers had got hold of the story and Anthony had found himself painted in them as the thuggish boyfriend and the main cause for the tragedy. Reporters had door-stepped him as he left and came home from work, shouting personal questions at him, making assumptions that there was more between Cynthia and himself than there were, trying to soil the beautiful memory of the woman that he loved.

The police had informed him that he was a key witness and had to be there for the trial, but he knew he had to get away from everything. The police had his mobile number and they could contact him if they needed him, but the open road beckoned him to assuage all his pain, to escape and help him to relax.

He carried on his journey to the next destination, a dot on the map. Over the past year he had moved around, not caring where he ended up, just finding somewhere to settle for a few weeks.

The smell of the sea air wafted on the light breeze, teasing his senses and drawing him closer to the small fishing village nestling in the crag of the cliffs that he had decided would be the next place to stay.

In a couple of months, he was due to return to give evidence at the trial, and this small village, isolated amongst the rolling hills was the turning point before working his way back to the last place on earth he wanted to be.

He drove his car to the harbor, parking it close to the small stone wall that edged the harbor entrance. Stomach starting to rumble, he realized it was time to grab something to eat and he twisted around looking up at the sprawl of buildings as they crawled up the side of the cliff that protected the village from the outside world.

Noticing a small café, he walked over to the old stone building, ignoring the small throng of families as they walked along the harbor area enjoying their day out in the quaint town.

Opening the chipped and battered wooden door, he ducked as he entered, moving from bright sunlight to a shadowy area where a handful of customers sat at red gingham covered tables chatting as they ate.

A large middle-aged lady with golden, brown hair stood behind the counter at the back of the room, an old fashioned wooden till sitting next to a vase with dried flowers that had seen better days.

Anthony walked between the tables towards the counter. The woman eyed him with interest and putting down the bag he brought with him on the floor next to him, he smiled and looked at the menu written in chalk on the blackboard set up on the wall.

Looking over the counter at the man standing in front of her, Brooke felt a spark of interest as she appraised the strong masculine body hugged by the tight white vest and worn blue jeans, smooth skin covered his wide muscled shoulders.

Unconsciously straightening her back so her ample chest, covered in the low cut bright yellow top lifted up, she smiled as she looked the man in the eye and inquired flirtingly, "Hello love, see anything you like?"

Anthony smiled back, instantly liking this straight forward, if a little over the top woman.

"Depends what you've got," He replied grinning at her obvious delight at his answer as she threw back her head and laughed.

"Darling, whatever you want,"

"A burger with fries would fill the gap right now, and a large cup of coffee,"

"Coming up, sit down and we'll bring it to you at your table," and shouting back through the door behind her to the kitchen, "Kim, burger and fry, and mug of coffee!"

Anthony found a table in front of the counter and sitting with his back to the woman, settled down to watch the people walking past the bay window at the front of the café as he waited for his food. People watching helped to clear his mind of all thought, and not really noticing at first the waitress as she walked up to the family sitting at the table to the right of the window, he stared blankly ahead.

Placing their drinks down in front of them, she bent slightly over, her small perky bottom encased in tight blue jeans pointing enticingly towards him.

Slowly his eyes glanced over her rear, his eyes following the line down from her bottom to her thighs and the stirrings of interest awoke in his groin. As she straightened up his glance swept up the length of her long slim back, and fascinated he watched as her shoulder blades, revealed by the shoestring straps of her clinging light blue camisole top, moved as she picked up some plates and placed them on the tray she held. A long black pony tail swung down her back, enticing as it pointed down in a dark thick column against her brown skin and the blue material of her top.

Feeling himself go harder, he shifted in his seat, and as she started to turn around, he looked up at her face wondering if she would be as beautiful from the front as she was from behind.

As she completed the turn, Anthony looked at her face and felt himself freeze with shock as he saw the brown almond shaped eyes and oval shaped face he had held in his heart and dreamt of each night since he met her.

Totally unheeding of the man sitting stock still at the corner table, Kimberly walked back to the kitchen and placing the tray load of plates on the counter moved over to the cook and picking up a fork turned the sausages and bacon over then stirred the baked beans before moving over to the small table behind her to butter a couple of slices of bread.

Anthony just sat there in shock, unsure of what he had seen. This woman was so like Cynthia it was uncanny, but there were subtle changes.

This woman had jet black hair, with a bang that hung down to her eyes, not the light brown silky hair that Cynthia wore framing her face. She had the same almond shaped eyes that he saw in his dreams, but now they were enhanced by black eyeliner, and heavy makeup defined her high cheeks and generous lips with blusher and lipstick. Large hoop earrings hung from her ears, brushing her shoulders and emphasizing her long slim neck. Somehow it looked like Cynthia, but it was if the picture was out of focus and not quite her.

Just then the woman behind the counter appeared at his side holding a knife and fork and placing them next to him on the table asked.

"On vacation love?"

"Uh no, just passing through," Finding it difficult to pull his mind away from Cynthia's double, he looked at the woman next to him, "I'm working my way around the US, and looking for temporary work and somewhere to crash. Do you know anywhere?"

"What type of work love?" then with a suggestive wink, "Although with those muscles, I should have thought anything physical would suit. I might have something if you're interested?"

Anthony looked at her not sure if she was being suggestive or serious. His mind was still on the vision he had just seen and asked, "What kind of something?"

"A little touching up here and there, some lifting and moving, a lot of stripping and tender loving care," and she laughed at the look on his face as she stood hands on hips.

"Clear that dirty mind my love, I own this little gem of a business, and as you can see it is a bit run down around the edges. This place needs a bit of painting and decorating if that's your thing. I won't pay you cash, but you can kip out the back in the spare room and have your food free as long as it takes you to get the place done,"

"It's a deal, if you include the burger as first payment." And putting out his hand they shook on the deal.

Just then Kim appeared, plate in hand, about to place it on the table in front of Anthony. Glancing up at the customer she was about to serve, shocked brown eyes met cold hazel ones, and with an involuntary gasp from her lips, the plate fell from her hands to the floor, food falling everywhere as the plate broke into pieces.

"Kim, what have you done!" the owner of the café said, not noticing the two people staring at each other, her young waitress in shock and starting to take a step backwards as she shook her head in disbelief.

A strong hand shot out and grabbing her wrist, pulled her forward, and in a low gravelly voice said, "Well, well, well, the walking dead. Hello, Cynthia. Long time no see."

Chapter 26

Brooke looked up from where she was
trying to gather up the bits of broken plate
and looked from the man sitting there; hand
around her waitress' wrist, eyes narrow, jaw
clenched his mouth a narrow slit, to the
young woman, a look of pure panic on her
face.

"You ok, Kim? Need any help? Listen
mister, I don't know what your problem is,
but we don't want any trouble here. I suggest
you let go of her wrist and we'll just call it a
day,"

Without taking his eyes from Cynthia's,
he quietly instructed her, "Tell her you're ok,
Cynthia. Tell her you and I are old friends
and need a little chat about old times,"

"My name is Kimberly and I don't take
shit from any man. Take your hand off my
wrist or I'll make sure you never get a
chance to get out of here in one piece," and
with her other hand she picked up the glass
ketchup bottle and held it up ready to hit
him on the head.

Suddenly, Anthony burst out laughing at the incongruous threat, and letting go of her wrist, his foot shot out under the table kicking the chair on the other side of the table back and nodding to it.

"Sit down Cynthia, I think it's time for you to explain why you left me living in hell for the past couple of months,"

Reassuring Brooke she would be alright, Cynthia slowly sat down as the worried older woman moved behind the counter keeping her eye on the two people sitting staring at each other.

After a long pause, each assessing the other, Anthony drew a deep breath and leaning back with arms crossed asked, "What did I do to you that made you leave me without even a word? I thought you were dead, we all did. Did you hate me that much that you couldn't say goodbye?"

"I don't owe you or anyone an explanation,"

"Oh, yes you do. The police will be very interested in knowing where you are,"

"You're not going to tell them. You can't let Eric know where I am,"

"I can't?" and leaning forward hissed, "He's in jail awaiting trial for your murder, and I've been to hell and back because of you. I loved you, I thought you were dead! I nearly went mad with grief, and you sit here calmly saying you don't owe me an explanation. Baby you owe me a lot more than an explanation,"

"I owe you nothing. I never promised you a thing. All men think they own women, but no one owns me. No man will ever own me again!" She exclaimed as she thought back on the night Anthony took her home.

Three months ago…

Cynthia groaned and turned on her back, her legs stretching out and hitting the leg of the kitchen table. Her head was pounding and the swellings and bruises on her face felt tight and throbbed painfully. Slowly, she moved her hand up to her head, gingerly touching the place where it felt like a spike was poking in her scalp and winced as her fingers found the wound and lump that was pulsating with every beat of her heart as the blood flowed through her body.

Uncomprehendingly, she looked at her fingers she had touched the wound with, seeing the blood staining her skin, sticky and wet, and laying there on her back on the cold floor, she sank back down into the sweet blackness of oblivion.

Cynthia didn't know how long she had laid there on the floor, it could have been minutes, or it could have been hours. Her body was aching, her head felt like a football that had been kicked repeatedly, throbbing and hot.

Carefully sitting up, wincing at the pain in her side where the chair had hit her, she looked around and grabbed the knife that had fallen from the counter. Her hand covered in blood, she gripped onto the knife as she listened frantically for any sign of Eric. After a while, she noticed that the house was too quiet, and he had to have *been gone. She placed the knife back down and tried to gather herself.*

She knew she had to get out at once, the need to save herself the most paramount emotion giving her the strength to get first to her knees and then to her feet as she staggered out of the kitchen to the front door.

Opening it, she carefully looked outside into the dark night, and pulling her blood smeared jacket tighter around her, she unsteadily walked out, closing the door to her home and her life behind her.

Shakily, she walked to the end of the road, not sure what to do or where she was going, moving slowly with her head down, and dazed with pain, her feet instinctively took her along, moving her step by step on the first leg of her new life, to the one place she really felt safe.

***

Cynthia lay curled up in a ball on the bed, tears streaming down her battered face, clutching the pillow to herself as the sobs wracked her body.

Last night without thinking, she had walked through the dark streets for over an hour, unaware where she was going, her head hurting and fuzzy, until coming to a halt as she realized she had walked across town to Mrs. Brown's house.

Going through the wooden gate, the one that Anthony had repaired that first week they met, and up to the front door, she stood there swaying, suddenly realizing she didn't have her handbag holding the keys to the house. She had left her home without taking a thing, no money, no keys, nothing but what she was standing up in.

Exhausted and staggering around to the back of the house she came to the kitchen back door and looking under the small pot holding a wilting plant that stood in a dark corner by the door, she picked up the small key she knew lay there, opened the back door, and entered the dark still house.

Moving around the house in the dark, and holding her aching head, the tears fell as *she realized she would never see the old lady again, but that even in death she had given Cynthia a gift, a sanctuary to run to while she gathered herself together and healed her wounds before the next step in her escape.*

Cynthia slept most of the day waking up late afternoon; she lay on the bed looking up at the ceiling above her, sad and neglected.

Her head throbbed, and one eye was partially closed where Eric's hand had managed to connect hard.

Climbing slowly off the bed, she limped across the room to look in the dressing table mirror. Body stiff and sore, she looked at herself, tears running down her cheeks, shoulders slumped.

Staring back at her was the image of a defeated woman, red bruise marks marred the smooth skin on her cheek and close to her eye, the lid slightly swollen, red and half shut, her hair matted and tangled, stained down one side with dried red blood.

Walking into the bathroom, she ran water into the old-fashioned claw footed bath tub and started to peel off her damp dirty bloodstained clothes, leaving them in a pile on the floor. A dark bruise had appeared across her ribs and arm where the chair had fallen on her, standing out as a livid dark mark against her brown skin.

Stepping into the tub and laying back in the hot water, she started to plan. She knew she could stay here at Mrs. Brown's for only a short while, maybe three to four days tops. It was such a short time to allow herself to heal and get back her strength before moving on.

There was a supply of tins of soup, biscuits and some dried food in the house and she could live of these without having to go out, and if she didn't turn on any lights at night, no-one would guess she was here.

Leaning back in the tub so that she could wash her hair, she winced as the water hit the split scalp and the lump lying under the surface. Gently she soaped herself clean, letting the hot water calm and warm her body, helping to relax and ease the aching in her bones.

Wrapping a towel around her slim body and one around her head, she stepped from the tub and padded out of the bathroom to find the clothes she had found left behind by Mrs. Brown's granddaughter, then walked down to the kitchen, avoiding the small opaque window at the front. Opening a kitchen cupboard, she found the biscuit tin and putting the kettle on stood remembering that day here in the kitchen, that first day when she met Anthony, and he reached up to get this very tin down.

The tears started to flow again as she realized she would never be able to see him again. Never sit quietly talking to him, listening to his stories, watching his smile as he thought of something that he found amusing, never have him gently tease her to make her smile, never feel his strong body as she leant against him, his warmth surrounding her and making her feel safe.

She needed to protect him from Eric at any cost. In her heart she believed what Eric had said, and that his need for revenge

would mean she could never be with
Anthony and put his life in danger.

Anthony looked across the table at the defiant woman, her back ramrod straight, her eyes glinting daggers at him, and then turning around to the café owner who was trying hard to overhear the heated exchange between them said.

"If your offer is still on, show me where I can dump my stuff and I'll get straight on with doing the repairs. Cynthia and I are going to reacquaint with each other, and it might take a little while for her to come up with a plausible story to spin me."

Getting up from the table, stepping over the food on the floor and grabbing his bag he followed Brooke out through the kitchen and the back door to a small stone storage room in the back yard.

"Listen here big man, I don't want any trouble. Kim is a good worker and it's the start of the season. Whatever is between the two of you behave yourself or you're out. I won't see her hurt. Do you understand?"

"Yeah, I understand, and the name is, Anthony,"

"Well, Anthony you can sleep on the cot in the store room, you'll find some tools in there, and I'll fix you a bacon sandwich and coffee. Start the repairs and leave your dealings with Kim until I close up. But remember one false move against her and you'll have me to deal with."

Stepping into the small room, Anthony looked around, tins and boxes of food was stored on shelves and piled up on a table in a corner. At the other end of the room was a fold up bed with a blanket on it and not much else except a couple of cardboard boxes full of odds and ends.

Dumping his bag on the bed next to where he sank down, he stared across the room not really sure of what had just happened. All the long months mourning her, blaming himself, dreaming about her, missing her, and here she was, holed up in this tiny little village in the middle of nowhere telling him she didn't owe him anything.

Still upset with her comment, he reacted without thinking and pulled out his phone to send a text.

I found her body.

To Be Continued…

Thank You So Much for Reading & Please
Leave A Review!!!

Please Like My Facebook Page

www.facebook.com/authorkamille

FIND MORE OF MY TITLES HERE:

www.amazon.com/author/kamille

Made in the USA
Las Vegas, NV
19 March 2023